'Fifteen men on the dead man's chest—
Yo-ho-ho, and a bottle of rum!
Drink and the devil had done for the rest—
Yo-ho-ho, and a bottle of rum!'

~The Pirates' Song, *Treasure Island*

Robert Louis Stevenson
TREASURE ISLAND
CAMPFIRE®
Classics
A Graphic Novel
Adapted by Andrew Harrar
Illustrated by Richar

TREASURE ISLAND

Robert Louis Stevenson

CAMPFIRE®

KALYANI NAVYUG MEDIA PVT LTD

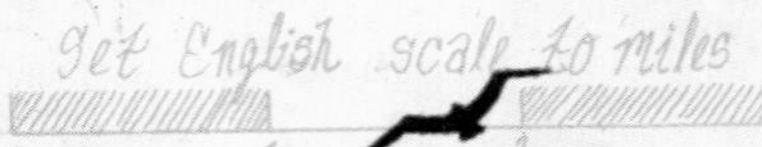

Robert Louis Stevenson

Wordsmith : Andrew Harrar
Illustrator : Richard Kohlrus
Colorist : Pawan Tiwary
Letterers : Bhavnath Chaudhary
Vishal Sharma
Editors : Suparna Deb
Divya Dubey

Cover Artists:

Illustrator : Richard Kohlrus
Colorist : Pawan Tiwary
Designer : Manishi Gupta

www.campfire.co.in

Mission Statement

To entertain and educate young minds by creating unique illustrated books that recount stories of human values, arouse curiosity in the world around us, and inspire with tales of great deeds of unforgettable people.

Published by Kalyani Navyug Media Pvt Ltd
101 C, Shiv House, Hari Nagar Ashram
New Delhi 110014
India

ISBN: 978-93-80028-21-7

Printed in India

About the Author

Robert Louis Stevenson was born in Edinburgh, Scotland in 1850. The son of an engineer, Stevenson followed in his father's footsteps by studying engineering and law at the University of Edinburgh. However, his passion for writing soon became more than a hobby, and he decided to pursue it on a full-time basis. This career choice initially upset his father, but Stevenson made a promise to complete his studies, and was admitted to the Scottish bar in 1875.

Stevenson's most famous work is the classic pirate tale *Treasure Island*, which was published in 1883. A fast-paced story of adventure, with mass appeal, it soon became popular across the world. In the 125 years since then, readers of all ages have delighted in following the exploits of young Jim Hawkins as he travels to a remote island in search of buried gold. Stevenson later created an infamous, but very intriguing, character in *The Strange Case of Dr. Jekyll and Mr. Hyde*, published in 1886. His adventure story *Kidnapped*, a tale of a young boy and a stolen inheritance, was also published in the same year. Throughout his life, Stevenson was frequently in poor health, and he often traveled abroad in search of places with mild climates. He also wrote a number of essays detailing these trips. During one such journey to France, he met an American woman named Frances Osbourne, and later married her during a visit to California.

In 1887, Stevenson headed for America with his wife, stepson and mother. He had become famous in New York, and received many attractive offers from various publishers. It was soon after this move that he took up his pen for *The Master of Ballantrae*, a novel which is considered one of his best works. Stevenson eventually settled with his family on the island of Samoa, where he died at the age of 44 on December 3, 1894. While best known for writing tales of action and adventure, Robert Louis Stevenson is also remembered as an accomplished poet and essayist.

Deadmans Cave
Shallow water
Spring
LONG JOHN SILVER
BILLY BONES
JIM HAWKINS
DR. LIVESEY
BEN GUNN
SQUIRE TRELAWNEY

Fifteen men on the dead man's chest—
Yo-ho-ho, and a bottle of rum!
My friends have asked me to write the story of Treasure Island. And I shall hold nothing back, except the location of the island, because treasure is still buried there.
I'll start at the time when my father owned the Admiral Benbow Inn, and an old sailor with a sword came to lodge under our roof.

This is a handy cove and a pleasant place to drink. Yes, it'll do just fine.
How long will you be staying, sir?
I'll stay for a while. You can call me Captain.
Sometimes, he would shock our country people with his dreadful stories about hanging, and walking the plank, and storms at sea, and the Dry Tortugas*, and wild deeds and places on the Spanish Main.
The gale nearly rolled our ship twice, and pirates attacked us the next morning!
And sometimes, he would sing his wicked, wild sea songs. I often heard the house shaking with 'yo-ho-ho and a bottle of rum'. Everyone would join in, scared for their lives.
*The Dry Tortugas are a small group of islands in the Gulf of Mexico.
What's your name, lad?
Jim Hawkins. My father owns this inn.
Keep an eye open for a seafaring man with one leg, and I'll pay you for your troubles.
Yes, Captain!
After that, on stormy nights, when the wind shook the house, the man with one leg haunted my dreams.

The man who stayed at the inn did not have the appearance of a common sailor. Instead, he seemed like a mate or skipper who was used to being obeyed.
I chose the perfect hiding spot.
Every time, when he came back from his daily stroll, he would ask if any seafaring men had passed by.
At first, we thought he was missing the company of other sailors. But then we realized he was actually trying to avoid them.
Our sailor guest is falling behind with his rent.
Month after month, he stayed on without paying a penny.
If you wish to continue staying--
I'll pay up tomorrow, good man.
I'm tired of your empty promises!
But, whenever my father mentioned it, the captain blew through his nose loudly and stared him out of the room.

My poor father soon fell ill.
Did the sailor pay his rent?
You need to rest, dear.
No, he keeps making excuses.
One afternoon, Dr. Livesey came to visit my father.
YO-HO-HO AND A BOTTLE OF RUM
Who is singing downstairs? It sounds like New Year's Eve!
The man you can hear is the one worrying my husband sick.
Don't fret. I'll soon be fine, dear.

After seeing my father, Dr. Livesey went into the parlor downstairs, while he waited for his horse.
Have you heard they have found a cure for rheumatics?
YO-HO-HO
...and a bottle of rum! Drink and the devil had done for the rest--
I can't hear myself talk with your mouth running like that.
Silence there, or I'll pin you to the wall!
Are you addressing me, sir? I have only one thing to say to you: if you keep on drinking rum, the world will soon have one less dirty scoundrel in it!
If you do not put that knife in your pocket this instant, I promise you shall hang at the next court session.

The captain was used to people living in fear of him, and it seemed that Dr. Livesey had taken him by surprise with his calm demeanor.
I am not only a doctor, but a magistrate, too. If I hear of any complaints against you...
...I'll have you hunted down, and turned out of this place.
Dr. Livesey, your horse is ready.
Not a moment too soon!
The captain held his peace that evening...
...and for many evenings to come.
Seen my one-legged friend, Jim?
Not a trace of him, Captain.
Good!

Not long after this, the first of a series of mysterious events occurred that got us rid of the captain. But that did not free us of his affairs.
INN
It was a bitter cold winter, with long, hard frosts and heavy gales.
My mother and I had the inn to ourselves, and we were kept busy, without having to pay much attention to our unpleasant guest.
Oooh!
My poor father's health deteriorated daily, and it was clear that he was unlikely to see the spring.
It was very early one January morning, when the captain set out down the beach.
How is Father?
Dr. Livesey will be coming to see him again today.
My mother was upstairs with my father, and, while I was laying the breakfast table...

...a man who I had never seen before walked in.
Is this table for my mate Bill?
No, it is for the man we call Captain.
My mate Bill would be called the captain. Is he here in this house?
No, he went out walking.
Which way did he go?
The stranger waited just inside the inn door, peering around the corner.
Here comes my mate. Let's give him a little surprise.
I felt very uneasy, and became alarmed as the stranger removed his sword from its sheath.

Bill, you remember your old shipmate, surely!
Black Dog!
You've run me down, and here I am. Well then, speak up. What do you want?
Bill, let's talk straight, like old shipmates.
Black Dog told me to leave the room.
For a long time, all I could hear was a low chattering sound.
But, at last, the voices began to grow louder, and suddenly there was a tremendous explosion of swearing. And the table and chairs went over with a crash.
You deserve a good thrashing, my old shipmate!
CRASH
A clash of steel followed...
Aaargh!
Let's put an end to this. If it comes to swinging, swing I say!
...and then a cry of pain...
Uhh!

...and the next instant, I saw Black Dog running away, and the captain chasing after him.
They should have called you Yellow Dog!
Black Dog, in spite of his wound, quickly disappeared over the edge of the hill in no time at all.
Jim! Rum! I must get away from here. I need rum.
Captain, are you hurt?
Just get the rum, laddie.
Uhhh.
Captain!
Dr. Livesey and my mother, alarmed by the cries, came running downstairs.
Dear me, what a disgrace upon the house! What shall we do?
You go upstairs to your husband, Mrs. Hawkins. I'll do my best to save this fellow's worthless life.

I fetched a basin of water for the doctor. When I returned, he had already ripped the captain's sleeve open, and exposed his great muscular arm.
Where's Black Dog?
There's no Black Dog here.
'Billy Bones' was tattooed on his forearm. And near his shoulder was a man hanging from some gallows.
You have had a stroke. Remember, rum means death for you. Now, Mr. Bones--
They're after my old sea chest. Old Flint gave it to me at Savannah when he was dying.
They'll have the black spot* on me soon.
What's that?
It's a summons.
*Whenever a piece of paper with a black spot in the middle was given to an accused pirate, it meant that he would be executed.
Can I get a mug of rum for a piece of gold?
The only money I want from you is what you owe my father. Here's one glass, but I'll get you no more.
Aye! Aye!

Your father is very ill, Jim. I'm afraid it's time to say goodbye.
My poor father died quite suddenly that evening, so all other matters were put to one side.
We are gathered here today...
MALONEY
My father's death filled me with sad thoughts.
We'll have to work harder now that your father is gone.
I'll do my best.
Here lies Interred the Body of M. HAWKINS who departed this life on JAN 13 Æ. 17
The funeral arrangements, and all the work at the inn, kept me so busy that I hardly had time to think of the captain, let alone be afraid of him.
Not long after that...
TAP TAP

...a dreadful-looking figure came to the inn.
Will any kind friend inform a poor, blind man where he is?
Ouch! You're hurting me. You are at the Admiral Benbow Inn, Black Hill Cove.
Now, boy, take me to the captain.
Sir, I dare not.
My name is Pew.Take me in right now, or I'll break your arm!
A friend is here for you, Captain.
Hold out your hand, Bill.
I had never heard such a cruel, cold and ugly voice as that blind man's.
I was so utterly terrified!
It was some time before either the captain or I managed to gather our senses.
Ten o'clock? I only have a few hours left. We'll do them yet.
Pew passed Bill something... a note.

The captain put his hand to his throat, swayed for a moment, and then, with a peculiar sound, fell back onto his bed.
Uhh...
Captain!
Mother, quick!
And with that, the blind man skipped out into the road.
The captain had been struck dead by a thundering stroke.
What shall we do, Mother?
We'll seek help from the neighborhood.
I lost no time in telling my mother all that I knew, and we realized we were in a difficult and dangerous position.
Nobody would agree to come to the Admiral Benbow. The more we told them about our troubles, the more they refused to leave the shelter of their houses.
We immediately ran out into the approaching evening and the frosty fog.
All I can do is lend you my gun and send word to the authorities. I'm sorry.
If none of you dare, Jim and I will deal with it ourselves. We will go back the way we came, and we'll open Billy Bones's chest, even if we have to die for it. No thanks to you, chicken-hearted men.

We went back home and found the note. It was a black spot. The captain had been given till ten o'clock that night.
Watch our backs from the hillside, Jones. Fire a warning shot at the first sign of trouble.
Draw down the blinds, Jim. They might come and watch from outside. We have to find the key to the chest.
I searched the captain's pockets, one after another. I found everything but the key, and began to despair.
Perhaps it's around his neck.
You're right. Here it is. Let's see if it opens the chest.
CLICK
A strong smell of tobacco and tar rose from inside. We searched through it and found little of value. When we got to the bottom, we found a bundle tied up in oilcloth, and a canvas bag that jingled with gold.
Take the whole bag, Mother, and let's be going.
I'll take what he owed us, and not a penny more.
This package seems strangely preserved. Could this be what the pirates are after?
We both stopped what we were doing. From the silent, frosty air outside came the sound of...

...the blind man's stick upon the frozen road. It brought my heart into my mouth.
TAP
TAP
The sound drew closer and closer while we sat holding our breath.
I can't see anything.
It's probably just the wind, Son.
Then something struck the inn door, and we could hear the handle being turned and the bolt rattling.
CHIK
And then there was silence for a long time.
At last, the tapping of the blind man's stick started again, and slowly died away.
Mother, take all of the money and let's leave.

I can see Pew—he's going back down to the cove!
I'll take the money I have.
And I'll take this. Let's go.
The Benbow is this way, lads!
The fog was rapidly dispersing, and the moon shone quite clear.
We must hurry!
We had not left a moment too soon.
My dear, take the money and run on. I think I am going to faint.
You rest. I'm going back for a quick look.
Those men are dangerous. Be very careful!
Bill's dead. Someone has emptied the chest, but left the money.
My curiosity was stronger than my fear. I crept back, hiding behind a bush, and watched what was happening at the inn.
Is Flint's fist there?
No, no sign of Flint's fist here.
ADMIRAL BENBOW
It's that boy. Search the house and find him.
There then followed a great search of our old inn, until the men came out and declared that we were nowhere to be found.
I wish I had put his eyes out. He must be close by.

I can hear Jones's signal for danger. Run for the boat!
KAPOW
You won't leave old Pew, will you, mates? Not old Pew!
Then came the sound of horses galloping, and the pirates turned and ran in every direction. One toward the sea, one across the hill, and so on.
Cut them off at the beach, men!
CLOP
CLOP
CLOP
In half a minute, no one was left but Pew.
They had deserted him.
Confused amid the flurry of sounds, Pew ran right into the path of Supervisor Dance's horse.
AAAAHHH!
Look out, man!

He tried to save Pew, but it was in vain.
AAAARRGH!
Supervisor Dance! It's me, Jim!
The thieves have escaped, sir.
Except for this poor fellow.
Pew fell on his side, then gently collapsed onto his face, and didn't move any more.
Supervisor Dance had come to our rescue. Without him, the pirates would surely have found us.
We left the Benbow behind and rode to Dr. Livesey's house.
One of my men has taken your mother to the station. She will be safe there.
Thank you, sir.
When we arrived, the doctor was with Squire Trelawney.
Good evening. How may we help you two?
We need to speak to you, sir.
Supervisor Dance and I told Dr. Livesey the whole story.
Thieves ransacked the Benbow Inn, and Jim thinks they were looking for this item.
You may leave now, Supervisor Dance. Thank you.
SNIP! SNIP!
Yes, sir!
The bundle contained two things—a book and a sealed paper.

The book had some scraps of writing in it—the type of thing a lazy man with time on his hands would write.
Flint's Log
Mr. W. Bones, Mate
It included dates and amounts and seemingly random words. The record that had been kept lasted for nearly twenty years. At the end of it was a grand total and, following that, the words 'Bones, his pile' appeared.
I can't make head or tail of this. Who is Flint?
He was the bloodthirstiest pirate that ever sailed!
Logs
And this is his account book. Now, what else do we have here?
The paper had been sealed in several places and the squire opened them with great care.
Let's have a look at this. Oh, my goodness!
What? What is it, man? Out with it!

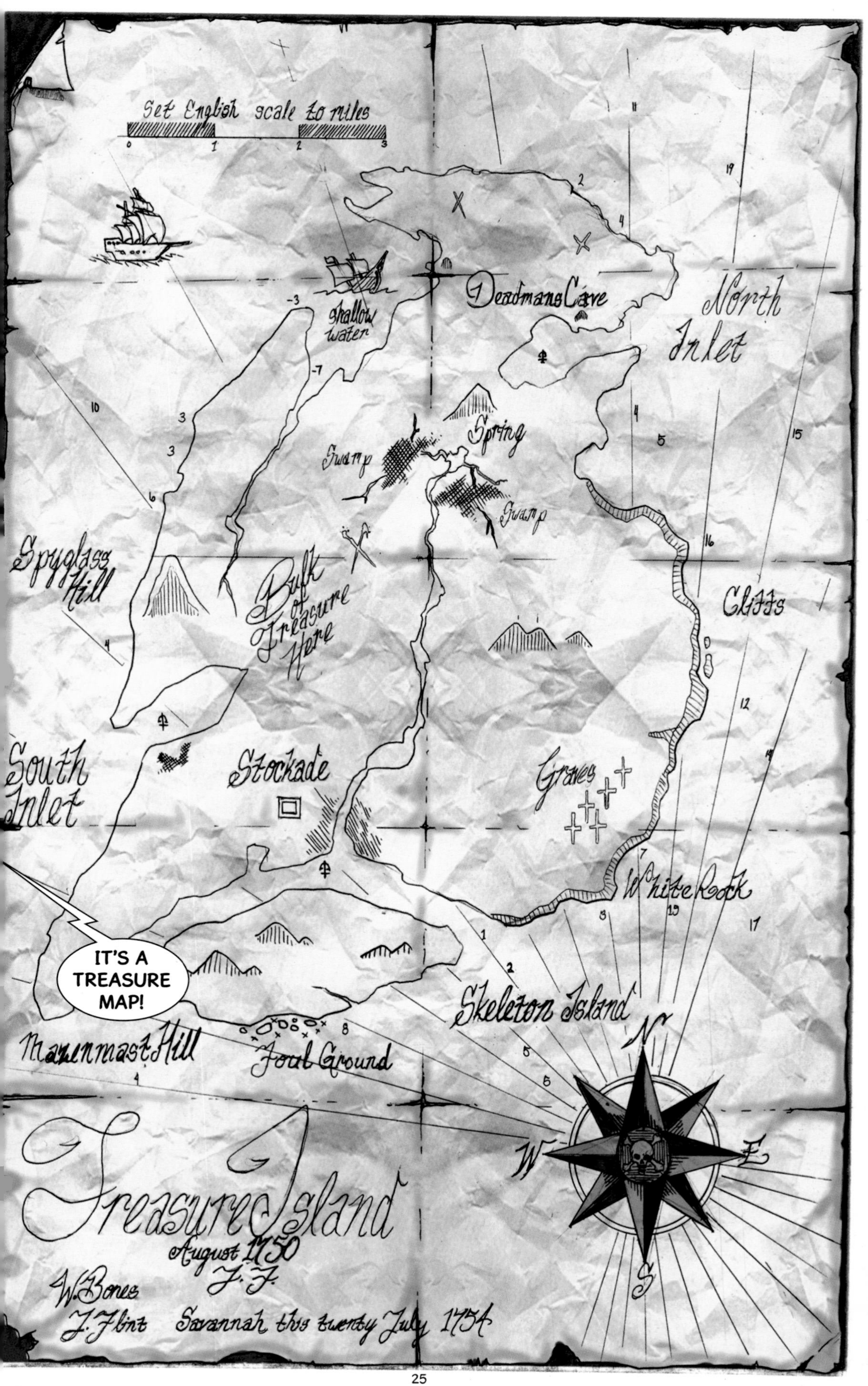
Set English scale to miles
Deadmans Cave
Shallow water
North Inlet
Spring
Swamp
Swamp
Spyglass Hill
Bulk of Treasure Here
Cliffs
South Inlet
Stockade
Graves
White Rock
IT'S A TREASURE MAP!
Skeleton Island
Mainmast Hill
Foul Ground
N
W
E
S
Treasure Island
August 1750
J. F.
W. Bones
J. Flint Savannah this twenty July 1754

It was a map of an island. And it was marked with the names of hills and bays and inlets...
This is the clue to where Flint buried his treasure. I'm going to get a ship ready.
...and every piece of information that we would need to bring a ship safely to its shores.
Livesey, you will give up your wretched doctor's practice at once.
On the back of the map, the same handwriting had added more information.
Tall tree, Spy-glass Shoulder
Bearing a point to N. of NNE
Skeleton Island E.S.E. and by E.
Ten Feet
The Bar Silver is in the North Cache
You Can Find it by the trend of the East hummock, Ten Fathoms
South of the Black Crag with a Face on it
The arms are easy found in the sand-hill,
North point of North Inlet Cape
Bearing E. and a quarter
It was brief and incomprehensible to me, but it filled the squire and Dr. Livesey with delight.
Tomorrow, I shall leave for Bristol. In ten days, we'll have the best ship and a first-class crew ready. You, Livesey, will be the ship's doctor, and I will be admiral.

Jim Hawkins, here, shall come as our cabin boy. And we'll take Redruth, Joyce and Hunter.
I'll go with you. But, there's only one man I'm afraid of.
And who's that?
You, for you cannot hold your tongue.
None of us must breathe a word of what we've found.
We're not the only men who know of this map.
I'll be as silent as the grave!
Those fellows who attacked the inn tonight are still on the loose. Have someone watch over Jim until we're ready to sail.
Woohoo. Treasure Island, here we come!
Treasure Island

Preparing to go to sea took much longer than the squire had imagined.
Doctor Livesey went to London to find a physician to look after his practice, while the squire was in Bristol getting things ready.
I stayed on at the hall under the supervision of old Tom Redruth, the gamekeeper. I was almost a prisoner...
Dear Livesey,
Our ship is ready. Her name is the Hispaniola. So now, you must not lose an hour and come fast. Jim should also go and see his mother
r one night with Redruth for a guard. Then, both of you should come full speed to Bristol.
John Trelawney
...but was full of sea dreams. The weeks passed by, till one day a letter arrived for Dr. Livesey. In his absence, I read it.
I was beside myself with glee.
We're off to Bristol, Tom!
Oh, I see.
The next morning, he and I set out on foot for the Admiral Benbow, and there I found my mother in good health.
Promise me you'll be careful!
Dr. Livesey and Squire Trelawney will be there too, Mother. Don't worry.

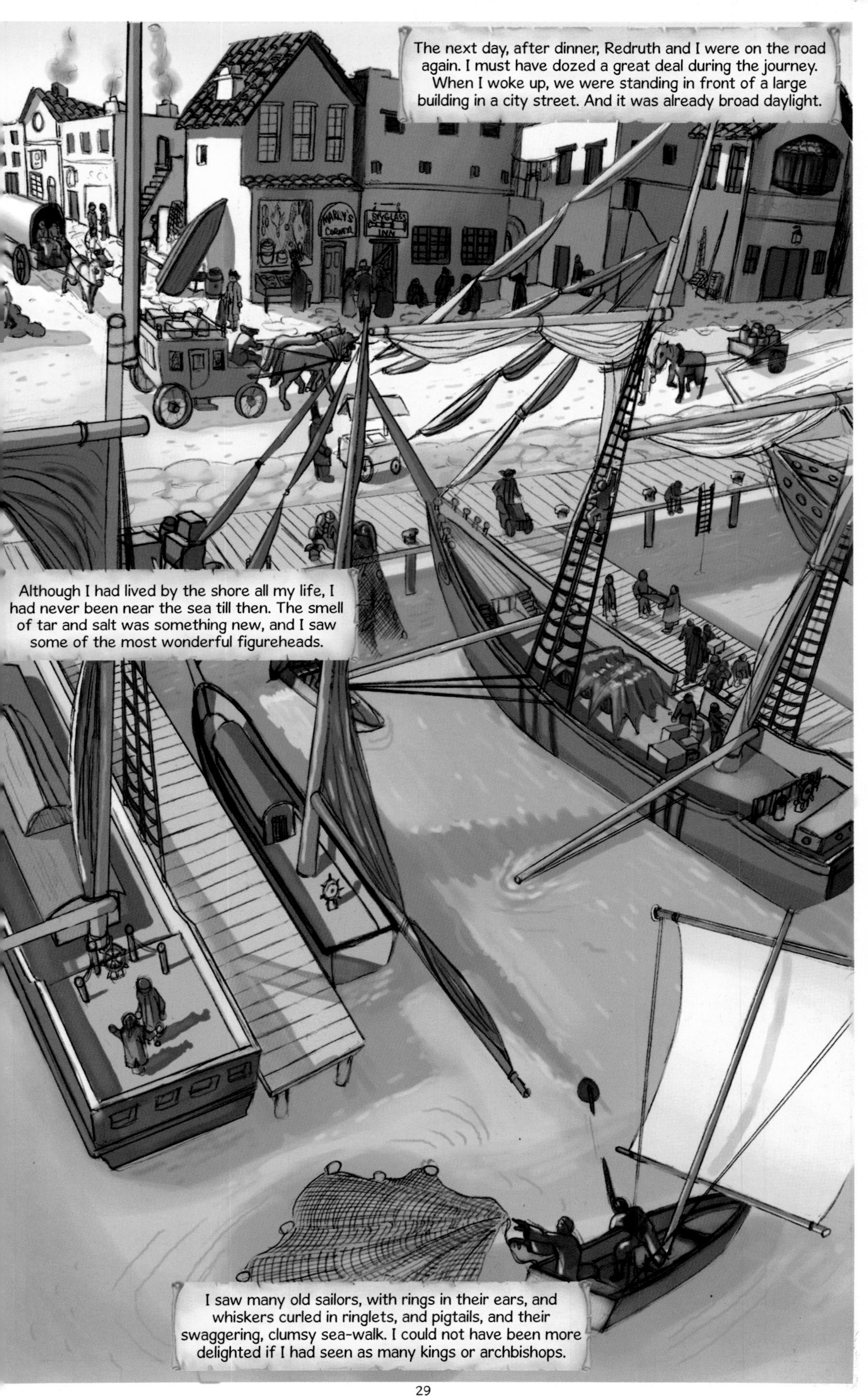
The next day, after dinner, Redruth and I were on the road again. I must have dozed a great deal during the journey. When I woke up, we were standing in front of a large building in a city street. And it was already broad daylight.
MARLY'S CORNER
SPYGLASS INN
Although I had lived by the shore all my life, I had never been near the sea till then. The smell of tar and salt was something new, and I saw some of the most wonderful figureheads.
I saw many old sailors, with rings in their ears, and whiskers curled in ringlets, and pigtails, and their swaggering, clumsy sea-walk. I could not have been more delighted if I had seen as many kings or archbishops.

Here you are. The doctor arrived last night too.
Bravo! The ship's company is now complete.
When do we set sail?
We sail at four o'clock tomorrow.
Will you deliver this note to Long John Silver? He's at the tavern.
What does he look like?
He's a friendly chap with a wooden leg.
John Silver
I was scared that he might be the same one-legged sailor that I had watched out for at the Benbow.
Mr. Silver, sir?
This couldn't be the same man, could it?
Yes, sir.
Yes, my lad. So you are our new cabin boy then?
I'm pleased to meet you.
Just then, a customer stood up and rushed to the door.

Stop him! It's Black Dog!
The rascal didn't even pay for his drink! Harry, run and catch him!
Aye, Silver!
One of the others, who was nearer to the door, leaped up in pursuit.
Have you seen Black Dog before, Morgan?
No, sir.
I used to see him here with a blind beggar.
I know the blind man, too. His name was Pew.
Blow me down! He robbed me three times over.
I lost him in a crowd, Silver!
No worries— we'll catch him next time.
Black Dog had got away, but nothing could be done.

Long John Silver was to be the ship's cook. And it was he, along with the squire, that had got the crew together. They were tough fellows, of unconquerable spirit.
The *Hispaniola* lay some way out. At last, however, we stepped aboard...
Welcome aboard, men!
...and were greeted by the mate, Mr. Arrow, a brown old sailor.
Before we had even set sail, the captain asked to meet with Squire Trelawney.
What do you wish to discuss, Captain Smollett?
Well, sir, I had better speak straight. I don't like this cruise. I don't like the men and I don't like my officer. There, that's short and sweet.

That's nonsense! Maybe you don't like the ship or your employer either?
I agreed to sail this ship wherever you want. But now I find out that every man on board knows more than I do.
I've learned we are going after treasure. I don't like treasure voyages, especially when they are secret.
And you don't like Mr. Arrow?
Mr. Arrow is a good seaman, but he is too friendly with his crew. A good officer should keep to himself.
So tell me, Captain, what do you want?
First, put all the weapons and gunpowder under your cabin.
Second, put your friends in sleeping berths next to you.
Anything more?
Yes, one more thing. I hear that you have a treasure map in your possession.
And then he named the exact latitude and longitude of Treasure Island.

The ship proved to be a good one, and the crew were capable seamen.
of rum?
He had no command among the men. After a day or two at sea, he began to appear on deck with hazy eyes, red cheeks, a stuttering tongue, and other marks of drunkenness.
And then one morning, he disappeared entirely.
Did you see him fall overboard?
No! But that saves us the trouble of putting him in irons. Officer Arrow was most incompetent.
Just after sundown, when all my work was over, I was making my way to my berth...
Hmm... are there any more apples?
Oops!
...when I had an accident.

I never told that to a soul!
The crew knows it, sir.
I am responsible for this ship's safety, so I am asking you to take certain precautions or let me resign from my position.
I will do as you desire, but I still think the worst of you.
You'll find I do my duty, sir!
We were hard at work, taking out the arms and changing the powder, when Long John Silver came aboard.
GUNPOWDER
Yo ho, mates! What's this?
We're changing the gunpowder, Jack.
Why? If we do that, we'll miss the morning tide!
My orders, Silver. You may go below, my man. Hands will want supper.
Aye, Captain!
All the crew respected and obeyed Long John Silver. He had a way of talking to them, and did everybody a particular service. To me, he was very kind, and always seemed glad to see me.
Looks like we have some rough sailing ahead.
She is, maybe, two hundred years old, Hawkins. She even sailed with the great Captain England once.
Stand by to go about!
She's handsome, Silver.
Pieces of eight! Pieces of eight!
me. Before I could lie down to snatch an hour of sleep, the *Hispaniola* had begun her voyage to the island of treasure.
Mr. Arrow, however, turned out even worse than the captain had feared.

That's nonsense! Maybe you don't like the ship or your employer either?
I agreed to sail this ship wherever you want. But now I find out that every man on board knows more than I do.
I've learned we are going after treasure. I don't like treasure voyages, especially when they are secret.
And you don't like Mr. Arrow?
Mr. Arrow is a good seaman, but he is too friendly with his crew. A good officer should keep to himself.
So tell me, Captain, what do you want?
First, put all the weapons and gunpowder under your cabin.
Second, put your friends in sleeping berths next to you.
Anything more?
Yes, one more thing. I hear that you have a treasure map in your possession.
And then he named the exact latitude and longitude of Treasure Island.

I never told that to a soul!
The crew knows it, sir.
I am responsible for this ship's safety, so I am asking you to take certain precautions or let me resign from my position.
I will do as you desire, but I still think the worst of you.
You'll find I do my duty, sir!
We were hard at work, taking out the arms and changing the powder, when Long John Silver came aboard.
Yo ho, mates! What's this?
We're changing the gunpowder, Jack.
Why? If we do that, we'll miss the morning tide!
My orders, Silver. You may go below, my man. Hands will want supper.
Aye, Captain!

was dog-tired when, a little before
lawn, the pipe was sounded and the
crew began to man the decks.
Fifteen men on the dead man's chest...
Yo-ho-ho, and a bottle of rum!
Off we go, mates!
Everything was new and interesting to me. Before I could lie down to snatch an hour of sleep, the *Hispaniola* had begun her voyage to the island of treasure.
Here's Captain Flint—that's what I call my parrot. Captain Flint was predicting success to our voyage, weren't you, Captain?
Pieces of eight! Pieces of eight!
She's handsome, Silver.
Stand by to go about!
She is, maybe, two hundred years old, Hawkins. She even sailed with the great Captain England once.
Looks like we have some rough sailing ahead.
All the crew respected and obeyed Long John Silver. He had a way of talking to them, and did everybody a particular service. To me, he was very kind, and always seemed glad to see me.

With the trade winds at our back, we made good time.
The ship proved to be a good one, and the crew were capable seamen.
Mr. Arrow, however, turned out even worse than the captain had feared.
Smollett thinks he steers better because I've drunk a few mugs of rum?
He had no command among the men. After a day or two at sea, he began to appear on deck with hazy eyes, red cheeks, a stuttering tongue, and other marks of drunkenness.
And then one morning, he disappeared entirely.
Did you see him fall overboard?
No! But that saves us the trouble of putting him in irons. Officer Arrow was most incompetent.
Just after sundown, when all my work was over, I was making my way to my berth...
Hmm... are there any more apples?
Oops!
...when I had an accident.

I fell asleep in the barrel and, on waking up, unintentionally overheard a conversation between Long John Silver and some of the crew.
I was too scared to show myself. I sat there, trembling and listening, with extreme fear and curiosity.
Flint was the captain, and I was the quartermaster. Flint's ships always came home full of gold. I was able to put two thousand in the bank after sailing with Flint.
Ah! Flint was the greatest pirate of them all.
Most gentlemen of fortune waste their money on drinks and gambling, but I've stashed away enough to live rather comfortably... and so can you.
I knew then that conspiracy was afoot and that the lives of all the honest men on board depended on me.
You're brave and smart. Why don't you join us?
Of course I will, Silver!
I think, if I could, I would have killed Silver through the barrel.
I must **warn** the others!

They were nothing more than common pirates.
The squire and the doctor have a map. Let them find the stuff and get it aboard.
Then we'll see. I'll finish with them at the island.
What are we going to do with them, Silver?
I vote for death! This time it's serious.
Wait is what I say. But when the time comes, let her rip!
John, you're a man!
You'll say so when you see what I do, Israel.
Now, Dick, you just jump up, and get me an apple.
Forget that, John. Let's have a go at the rum instead.
You can imagine the terror I felt. I would have leaped out and run for it if I had found the strength. But my body and my heart both failed me.
As terrified as I was, I couldn't help thinking that this must have been how Mr. Arrow was destroyed.

Just then, a sort of brightness fell upon me in the barrel. The moon had risen and was shining silver on the mast and white on the edge of the foresail.
Land ho!
In an instant, I slipped out of the barrel, and came out upon the deck.
Men, have any of you seen that land ahead before?
I know this place. It's called Skeleton Island. I was on a trader ship that was here once. It used to be the main place for pirates.
I have a chart here. See if that's the place.
Yes, sir. This is the spot to be sure, and very prettily drawn too.
This is not Billy Bones's map. Everything is marked except for the treasure!
Thank you, my man. I'll ask you to help us later on. Now, you may go.
I was surprised at the coolness with which John spoke of his knowledge of the island. I had, by this time, been horrified by his cruelty, deceit and power.

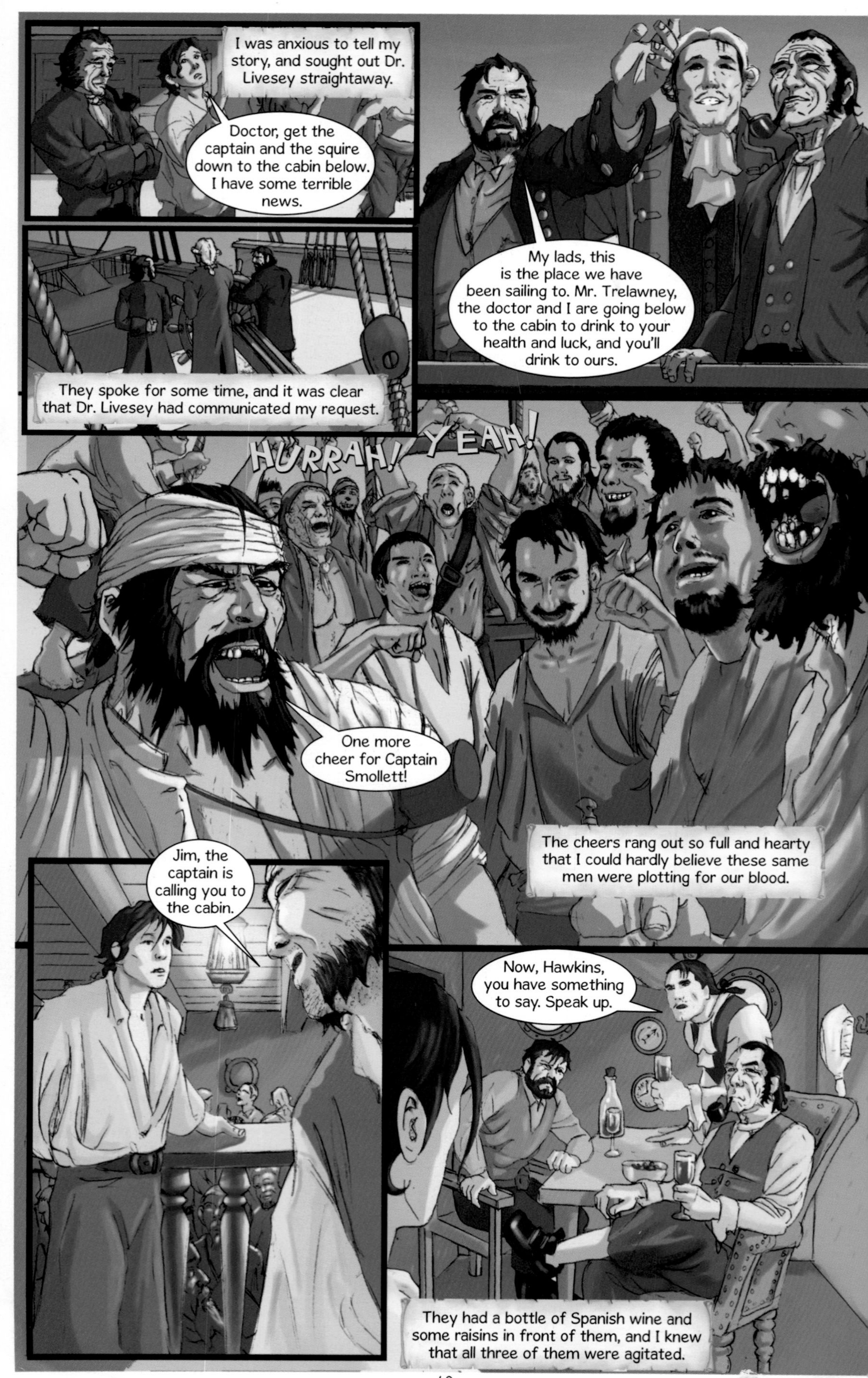
I was anxious to tell my story, and sought out Dr. Livesey straightaway.
Doctor, get the captain and the squire down to the cabin below. I have some terrible news.
They spoke for some time, and it was clear that Dr. Livesey had communicated my request.
My lads, this is the place we have been sailing to. Mr. Trelawney, the doctor and I are going below to the cabin to drink to your health and luck, and you'll drink to ours.
HURRAH! YEAH!
One more cheer for Captain Smollett!
The cheers rang out so full and hearty that I could hardly believe these same men were plotting for our blood.
Jim, the captain is calling you to the cabin.
Now, Hawkins, you have something to say. Speak up.
They had a bottle of Spanish wine and some raisins in front of them, and I knew that all three of them were agitated.

I did as I was asked, and told them the details of Silver's conversation. Nobody interrupted me till I was done.
Now, Captain, you were right and I was wrong. I admit I am an ass, and I await your orders.
You are no more an ass than I, sir.
I never met a crew that planned to mutiny but showed no signs beforehand. This crew beats me. I have three points and, with Mr. Trelawney's permission, I'll name them.
You, sir, are the captain. Please speak.
First point—we must go on, because we can't turn back. If we did, Silver's men would rise at once.
Second point—we have time, at least, until this treasure is found.
Third point—it's got to come to blows sooner or later. I suggest we attack them when they least expect it.
And to think they're all Englishmen! Sir, I would like to blow the ship up.
SLAM
Well, gentlemen, we must keep a lookout for any signs.
Jim here can help us more than anyone. The men are not shy with him.
I began to feel pretty desperate. Yet, under strange circumstances, it was indeed through me that safety came.

The appearance of the island, when I came on deck the next morning, was completely different. We were now lying just to the south-east of the low eastern coast.
Although there was hardly any breeze, we had covered a great deal of distance during the night.
Woods covered a large part of the surface, and the general coloring was uniform and sad.

Perhaps it was because of the way the island looked—
with its melancholy trees, and wild stone spires, and
with the surf foaming and thundering on the beach—
that I hated the very thought of Treasure Island.
You would have thought anyone would have been glad to
get to land after being at sea for so long. Yet, my heart
sank into my boots at the first sight of this island.

There's rebellion in the air.
What's next?
Let's give our crew the afternoon off. They will come back again as mild as lambs.
My lads, we've had a hot day and are all tired and out of sorts. Let's go ashore for the afternoon.
I'll fire a gun half an hour before sunset. Then we will return to the boats!
Six fellows stayed on board, and the remaining thirteen, including Silver, began to embark.
I decided to go ashore quietly.
I'm sick of rowing!
And I'm terribly thirsty!
No one took any notice of me.
The crew raced for the beach. The boat I was in shot far ahead of the other one. As soon as the bow struck shore, I jumped out.
Jim! Jim!
I paid no attention to him. Making haste, I ran straight ahead, till I could run no longer.

Meanwhile, back on the ship...
I wish Jim hadn't run off like that! I hope he is safe.
Waiting was a strain on those left on board. So Dr. Livesey and Hunter decided to go ashore in search of information.
We shouldn't land near those thugs.
Which way, Dr. Livesey?
We shall head toward the stockade.
Back on the island, I discovered it was uninhabited. I ran away from the pirates so hard and fast that I got lost.
There was nothing left for me but death by starvation or death at the hands of the rebels.
SSSSSSSSS
Suddenly, I heard a sound.
SNAP
Who goes there?
A figure leaped behind the trunk of a tree with great speed.

Who are you?
I am poor Ben Gunn. I haven't spoken to a Christian in the last three years.
Three years! Were you shipwrecked?
No, mate—marooned.
I knew the word marooned meant a horrible kind of punishment. It was common among pirates, and was when the offender was put ashore with some powder and shot, and left behind on an island.
What do you call yourself, mate?
Jim.
Did you come in Flint's ship?
No. Flint is dead, though some of his old crew are aboard.
Meanwhile, on the other side of the island, Dr. Livesey had found the stockade.
Once inside, you could hold off a small army.
Or a band of pirates. I think this is the spot for us.
AAARRGH!
Good heavens! I hope that wasn't Jim!

Consider this a warning to anyone who dares to defy me.
It wasn't me. It was Tom, one of the honest men. Long John Silver had killed him because he had refused to join the mutiny.
Back on board the *Hispaniola*, Silver's crew were being detained by Captain Smollett and Squire Trelawney.
Mr. Hands, there are two of us here with one pistol each. Please go below deck.
What? Silver will hang you!
Hurry, dogs!
These faint-hearted seamen were completely taken aback and they didn't make a sound.
We're not leaving any weapons for Silver.
Captain. I'm with you, sir. I'm not a pirate.
That's a wise decision, Mr. Gray.
Dr. Livesey returned to the *Hispaniola*. Then he and his men left for the stockade again, taking the arms with them.

Back on the island, I followed Ben Gunn.
I hope a man with one leg did not come with you?
Do you mean Long John Silver?
Aye, Silver! That was his name.
I told him the whole story of our voyage and the situation we found ourselves in.
He listened to me with the keenest interest and, when I had finished, he patted me on the head.
You're a good lad, Jim. Now, I'll tell you something. I was in Flint's ship when he buried the treasure.
Flint took six strong seamen on shore with him and came back to the ship alone. All six were dead—dead and buried. We left the treasure there, and set sail to get more.
Three years back, I came here in another ship. After twelve days of searching in vain for Flint's treasure, my captain left me here alone with a spade, a pickax and a musket. He told me to keep looking!
I have more confidence in a born gentleman than in these gentlemen of fortune, having been one myself.
Well, I don't understand a word you've been saying. But that's neither here nor there. Now, how am I going to get back on the ship?

Well, here's my boat, which I made with my own hands. If the worst comes to the worst, we can escape in it after dark. How's that?
At that moment, we heard some cannon shots followed by the sound of many guns.
They're fighting already!
Stay under the trees, Jim!
KA-BOOM!
When Dr. Livesey and the others had started heading for the stockade again, the pirates left on the ship decided to sink his little boat.
KA-BOOM!
Feed me another round, mates!
Although they had removed all the small arms, Dr. Livesey and his men had forgotten about the cannon and the powder left behind on the ship.
'hey've changed their course. They're showing us their broadside. Now is the time to hit them. Quick!
BOOM!
SPLASH
Row faster!
We can't without sinking her. Don't steer us in yet; the current's too strong.
We could be in trouble. Israel is manning the cannon and he was Flint's gunner.

Who's our best shot with the gun?
Squire Trelawney.
Mr. Trelawney, will you please kill one of those men, sir? Hands, if possible.
KRACK
The squire raised his gun, and the rowing ceased. Everyone leaned to the other side to keep the balance. It was so nicely planned that not a drop of water went into the boat.
Hands was the most exposed. However, just as Trelawney fired, Hands moved and one of the others fell instead.
Uhh!
The cry he gave was echoed, not only by his companions on board, but by a great number of pirates from the shore. They had started tumbling into their boats and were on their way back.

Where the next cannonball passed, nobody knew. It must have traveled over the heads of Dr. Livesey's party...
WHOOSH
We're sinking!
Grab what you can!
...and the wind it caused must have contributed to the disaster.
At any rate, the boat sank in three feet of water.
We've lost three guns!
Forget them and run for shore.
No great harm had been done. No lives were lost, and Dr. Livesey and his men were able to wade ashore safely.
They quickly made their way toward the stockade and, as they did, the voices of the approaching pirates got louder.
SNAP
We've got company, lads!
Shoot them dead!
KRACK
KRACK
Suddenly, seven pirates appeared in full cry at the south-western corner of the stockade.

The pirates paused as if taken aback and, before they could recover, Dr. Livesey, Squire Trelawney, Hunter and Joyce started to fire.
BLAM
One of the enemy fell...
...four shots were fired...
KRACK
...and the rest of the pirates turned and plunged into the trees.
They have more guns! Retreat!
Dr. Livesey's men started to rejoice over their success.
They weren't expecting that, were they!
Ha ha!
Just at that moment, a pistol cracked in the bush.
KRACK

A ball whistled past Dr. Livesey's ear... and poor Tom Redruth got hit.
Uhh!
Both the squire and Dr. Livesey returned fire, but there was nothing to aim at.
Am I dying, Doctor?
Tom, my man, you're going home.
Tom, say you'll forgive me.
Would that be respectful of me, Squire? So be it, amen!
It's the custom, sir, to read a prayer. Would one of you do it?
And not long after, without another word, he passed away.
How long before a rescue ship is sent?
Six months at the minimum.
We won't last that long.

We don't have much food. It's a pity we lost the second load, sir.
As for powder and shot, we'll manage. But the rations are short—so short, Dr. Livesey, that perhaps we're better off without that extra mouth.
Thankfully the stockade is right next to a spring.
I say. It's time to raise our flag.
Captain Smollett attached the flag to a tree branch, and set it on the roof.
This seemed to relieve him.
Just then, a round shot passed high above the roof of the log house.
Oho! Blaze away, you lousy pirates! You've little powder left anyway!
WHOOM

They're aiming for the flag. Would it not be wiser to take it down?
Strike my colors! No sir, not I!
The aim of the second shot was better, but the ball knocked down a tree, doing no further damage.
CRASH
Dr. Livesey! Captain!
Hello, Jim!
I had reached the stockade safe and sound.
We thought we'd lost you, Jim!
No, sir!
Good—we now have more eyes for guard duty.
Tom was buried before supper, as we didn't know when the pirates would return.
I'm going to miss Tom.

Silver's men stole some of our supplies!
The devils!
The pirates were bolder than we had expected.
...and then I met Ben Gunn. I am not very sure whether he's sane.
Not surprising, considering the circumstances.
As we had supper, ball after ball flew over or fell short or kicked up the sand in the enclosure.
One ball popped in through the roof of the log house and landed on the floor.
I rather dislike uninvited guests!
CRASH
All through the evening, they kept thundering away.
We soon got used to that sort of horse-play and did not mind it any more.

YO-HO-HO AND A BOTTLE OF RUM
Even though we were about half a mile away, we could hear the pirates roaring and singing late into the night.
Their numbers had been reduced from nineteen to fifteen, and two were wounded—one severely.
I was woken up the next morning by a bustle, and the sound of voices.
Flag of truce!
It was Silver himself.
It was still quite early, and the coldest morning ever.
And what do you want with your flag of truce?
To come on board and state terms.
I've come to get the treasure map that you have.
You won't get a thing!
You can come aboard along with us, once the treasure is found. I'll give you my word of honor, that I'll leave you somewhere safe. Or, if you want, you can stay here.
I don't trust you, Silver. Get out of here, now.
Fine then. But before the hour's out, I'll blow away your log house. Those who die will be the lucky ones.

You'll never find the treasure. And you won't be able to sail away. There's not a man among you fit to sail the ship.
You're making a big mistake!
And with a dreadful oath, Silver stumbled off.
My lads, we're outnumbered. I don't need to tell you that. But we have the advantage of fighting from shelter. I am sure we can defeat them.
Captain Smollett then told us his plan for defense.
Each of us stood guard at our posts.
Hang them! This is as dull as the doldrums.
An hour passed, with no sign of the pirates. But then...
KRACK
Here they come!
To your stations!
POW
...several bullets struck the log house, but not one entered.
How many on your side, Livesey?
Three shots were fired from this side, Captain.
And how many on yours, Squire Trelawney?

Hard to say on this side. Eight or nine at least.
Let's give them another round of firing, mates!
KRACK
Good heavens!
Suddenly, a bullet knocked the doctor's gun into bits.
BLAM BLAM
Arghh!
Ugh!
And a cloud of pirates leaped from the woods. They began to swarm over the fence like monkeys.
They're no match for us in close combat!
All hands at them—all hands!
POW
They made straight for the building, shouting as they ran. In a moment, they were upon us.

Our position was utterly reversed.
THUD
A moment before, we had been undercover, firing at an exposed enemy. But now it was us who lay uncovered, and could not fight back.
One pirate attacked the doctor.
ARRGH!
Out lads, out. Fight them in the open! Get your swords!
BLAM BLAM
The log house was full of smoke, which gave us an element of safety.
I got a slash on my knuckles as I went to pick up a sword from the pile.
Around the house, lads! Around the house!
BLAM POW
And suddenly, I was face to face with Anderson.
Say goodbye, mate!
No!
He roared aloud, as he prepared to bring his sword down upon me.

had no time to be afraid.
I leaped to one side, rolling headlong down the slope.
By the time I recovered, the victory was ours.
KA-BAM
Uhh!
Fire—fire from the house! And you, lads, back into cover!
We ran full speed for shelter.
Gray had cut down one, another had been shot dead, and Dr. Livesey had disposed of a third.
By this time, the house was clear of smoke, and we could see the price we had paid for victory.
Hunter's dead.
Joyce had also been shot through the head, never to move again.
We got five of the pirates.
That leaves nine of them, and gives us better odds than we had at the start.

The pirates did not return that day.
Your shoulder blade is cracked, but it's not serious.
I wish I could say the same for Hunter.
We had time to overhaul the wounded, and get dinner ready.
Stay here. You mustn't walk or move your arm.
Where are you going?
I'm off to see Ben Gunn.
Dr. Livesey is lucky. He gets to walk in the cool shadow of the woods, while I am stuck doing hard labor.
I started to hate being confined to that stockade. I felt disgust for the place, that was almost as strong as fear.
This disgust kept growing stronger and stronger, till at last I took the first step toward carrying out the foolish act I was planning.

The scheme I had in my head wasn't a bad one.
First, I went to find Ben Gunn's coracle.
Then, I slipped out under the cover of night, and made my way toward the *Hispaniola*.
Soon I reached the ship's hawser. My plan was to cut her adrift and let her go ashore where she pleased.
The hawser was as stiff as a bowstring. And the current was so strong, that the ship pulled upon her anchor.
SNIKK
With my knife, I cut one strand after another...
...till the vessel was nearly free.
Uhh!
SNAP
I waited for the breeze to come again and, when the hawser became loose, I cut the last fibres.

I then began to hear the sound of loud voices from the cabin.
CRASH
SMACK
I can't really say why I took hold of that cord. I suppose curiosity got the better of me.
Through the window, I saw two men arguing fiercely. On of them was Israel Hands.
You drunk fool!
Both men were not only drunk, but also furiously angry.
ARGH!
My scheme complete, I set off for the shore in my coracle.
The joke's on you now, Silver!
Alas, the current began to carry me away. I heard noises from the ship and knew that the pirates had been awakened to a sense of disaster.
Scared of being caught, I lay low in the skiff for hours.
Gradually, my weariness grew, until sleep overcame me.

It was broad daylight when I woke up and found myself at the south-west end of Treasure Island.
The current was still too strong for me to control my coracle, and I was not able to land on the rocks.
I don't like the idea of trying to land on these rocks and having to face these fearsome looking creatures. I'll try to paddle around to a safer part of the island.
The current carried me to the next reach of open sea, and there in front of me was the *Hispaniola*.
It was clear that nobody was steering the ship.
Either they were drunk or had deserted her.
If I can paddle up to the ship, I could easily take control of her.
I managed to bring myself up close to the *Hispaniola*.
As I climbed, a dull blow told me that the *Hispaniola* had struck my coracle. I was left without retreat.

The two pirates who I had spied on earlier were there. O'Brien was dead, while Israel Hands was moaning. They had tried to kill each other in their drunken wrath.
Brandy.
I found a bottle of brandy for Hands.
I've come aboard to take possession of this ship, Mr. Hands. You'll regard me as your captain till further notice.
Aye, by thunder, I needed that.
I can't have these colors, Mr. Hands. Better none than these.
God save the king! And there's an end to Captain Silver!
I believe, Captain Hawkins, you'll want to get ashore. Now, let's talk.
Some of the color had come back into Hands's cheeks, but he still looked very sick.

You give me food and drink and I'll tell you how to sail her.
Okay, let's head for the north inlet and put her ashore there.
We struck our bargain on the spot.
In three minutes, I had the *Hispaniola* sailing easily along the coast of Treasure Island.
I was very happy with my new command, and pleased with the bright, sunny weather and the prospects of the coast.
Tell me, Jim, do you think a dead man is as good as dead or does he come alive again?
You can kill the body but not the spirit, Mr. Hands. O'Brien there is in another world, and may still be watching us.
Well, that's unfortunate. Looks like killing him was a waste of time.
Jim, can you bring me a bottle of wine? This brandy is too strong for my head.
Some wine? White or red?
Any, as long as it's strong and there's plenty of it.
All right, I'll bring you port wine, Mr. Hands. But I'll have to look for it.
I didn't believe the idea of him preferring wine to brandy. The whole story was an excuse. He wanted me to leave the deck.
I quietly returned to spy on my companion.
Where's my knife?

Here's the wine, as you wanted.
But if I were you, and thought badly of myself, I would say my prayers like a good Christian.
Why do you say so?
You've broken your trust. You've lived in sin, and lies, and blood. There's a man you killed lying at your feet right now, and you ask me why! For God's mercy, Mr. Hands, that's why.
For 30 years I've sailed the seas, and seen good and bad, better and worse, fair weather and foul.
And I tell you, I've never seen good come out of goodness yet. I believe in him who strikes first. Dead men don't bite, that's my view.
I was steering the boat. At Hands's command, I put the helm hard up. The *Hispaniola* swung quickly, and headed for the shore.
With all the excitement of bringing the ship to shore, I had forgotten the danger I was in.
Arhh!
No!

I leaped sideways, just in time.
Uhh!
Before Hands could recover, I got out of the corner, which gave me all the deck to dodge about.
I stopped and drew a pistol from my pocket.
CLICK
Huh?
Your lucky day, Jim!
There was neither a flash nor a sound. The thing was useless thanks to the sea water.
With the pistol failing me, I decided on a different course of action.
Despite his wounds, Hands could still move fast.
I had two more pistols on me and, when I had a moment, I got them both ready.
One more step, Mr. Hands, and I'll blow your brains out. Dead men don't bite, you know.
As you'll soon find out!

Then, suddenly...
Uhh!
BLAM
...he pinned me to the mast by my shoulder. And in the surprise of the moment, both my pistols went off.
SPLASH
My wound pained me a good deal and bled freely, but it was neither deep nor dangerous.
Hngh!
I dropped both my pistols and they fell into the water along with Israel Hands.
Leaving the *Hispaniola* by the bay, I moved away from the sea.
I was anxious to get home to the stockade and boast of my achievements.
There was no doubt they kept a bad watch.
PECK
If it had been Silver and his lads who were now creeping in on them, not one of them would have seen daybreak.
ZZZZZZZZ
PECK
PECK
It was completely dark. However, I could hear the steady drone of the snorers and a small occasional noise—a flickering or pecking that I could not understand.

The worst of my fears had come true. The pirates were in possession of the house and the stores.
Pieces of eight!
Nice of you to drop by.
Where are my friends?
I stood there, looking Silver in the face with black despair in my heart.
Dr. Livesey wanted to bargain because the old ship was gone.
So, we bargained. And here we are with the stores, the brandy and the log house. As for them, I don't know where they are.
My fate is in your hands but, I must tell you, I have been on top of this business from the beginning.
Death to the cabin boy!
Don't interrupt! Let him finish.
It was I who overheard you on the ship and alerted the others.
It was I who cut the *Hispaniola's* anchor to set her free.
Kill me if you please. But, if you let me live, I'll do my best to spare your lives from the gallows.

I'm the captain here. I'll not let you lay a hand on him.
We need to step outside for a council.
All the pirates marched out, and left Silver and me alone.
I know when a game's up, Jim. I'm on your side now. I say to myself, you stand by Hawkins, and Hawkins will stand by you.
You mean all is lost?
I do. Once I saw the ship was gone, I realized it was over. So, Jim, I'll save your life from them. But, you save Long John from swinging.
What I can do, I'll do.
The pirates returned with a black spot.
You're over now, Silver. You'll step down as captain.
That black spot isn't worth anything.
You made a hash of this cruise, and then you let the enemy leave here for nothing.
Not quite. I made a bargain for food... and this.
I recognized the chart instantly.

This is Flint's—
sure enough.
Yes. You lost the ship and I found the treasure. So, who's the better man?
Why the doctor had given it to him, I could not understand.
Early the next morning, the doctor showed up.
I'm here to see any of your patients.
Dr. Livesey proceeded with his work for the sick.
So, Jim, here you are. You have to face the consequences of your actions, my boy. It was cowardly of you to go off like that.
Doctor, I have blamed myself enough. My life is forsaken already. I would have been dead by now if Silver hadn't stood up for me.
I got the ship, Doctor, partly by luck and partly by taking risks. She lies in the north inlet on the southern beach.
There is a kind of fate in this. At every step, it's you who saves our lives. So, how can we let you lose yours?

Silver! Hear my advice. Don't be in a hurry to look for the treasure.
Right after breakfast, the pirates set off in search of the treasure.
What do you mean?
I can't say any more. It's not my secret, Silver, or I'd tell it to you. I'm off to find help for you.
And with those words, Dr. Livesey headed into the woods.
We'll locate the treasure first, and then find our ship.
And off to sea like jolly companions.
The treasure will be found near a tall tree, bearing to a point of north by north east.
Can anyone see this tree we're looking for?
I sight one!
We began to climb the slope toward a plateau.
After about half a mile, we were quite close to the brow of the hill.
Once at the top, we found a human skeleton that lay on the ground.
He was a sailor.
He is pointing north toward the treasure!
Flint always loved a joke.
I believe a chill struck every heart for a moment.

All of a sudden, a thin, high, trembling voice struck up the well-known words.
FIFTEEN MEN ON THE DEAD MAN'S CHEST - YO-HO-HO AND A BOTTLE OF RUM!
DARBY M'GRAW! FETCH THE RUM, DARBY!
Those were Flint's last words. It must be his ghost. Run!
That's no ghost. There was an echo. There are no spirits that have an echo.
Dick had his bible out.
BIBLE
Well, you're right, John. It didn't sound like Flint's voice. It was like somebody else's voice. It was like--
It was like Ben Gunn's voice.
Nobody is scared of Ben Gunn, dead or alive.

Hearing no more sounds for a while, the men shouldered their tools and set off again.
We'll keep on, now, till we find the treasure.
Slow down, Jim! I can't keep up with you!
Silver hobbled along, grunting, on his crutch.
The first two tall trees we came to were not the one on the map.
I'm sick of looking for tall trees, Silver.
But my companions finally located the right tall tree. They were very excited that seven hundred thousand pounds lay in its shadow.
It's digging time, gentlemen of fortune.

After digging for several hours...
Well, blow me down!
The seven hundred thousand pounds, all gone.
...it was very clear; the treasure had been found and taken away.
Each of the men was shocked. But with Silver, the blow passed almost instantly.
WALRUS
Every thought of his soul had been set on that money. But he kept his head and his temper, and adjusted his plan before the others had had time to realize their disappointment.
The pirates, with oaths and cries, began to leap, one after another, into the pit, and to dig with their fingers.

I found two guinea coins. That's your seven hundred thousand pounds, is it?
You knew it was empty all along, didn't you, Silver?
Jim, take that, and stand by for trouble.
A boy and a cripple are really no match for us! Now, mates--
He was raising his voice, and was about to charge. But, before he could...
BLAM
CRACK
CRACK
...shots flashed out of the bushes.
Aaargh!
Uhh!
Two of the pirates fell dead. The other three turned and ran with all their might.

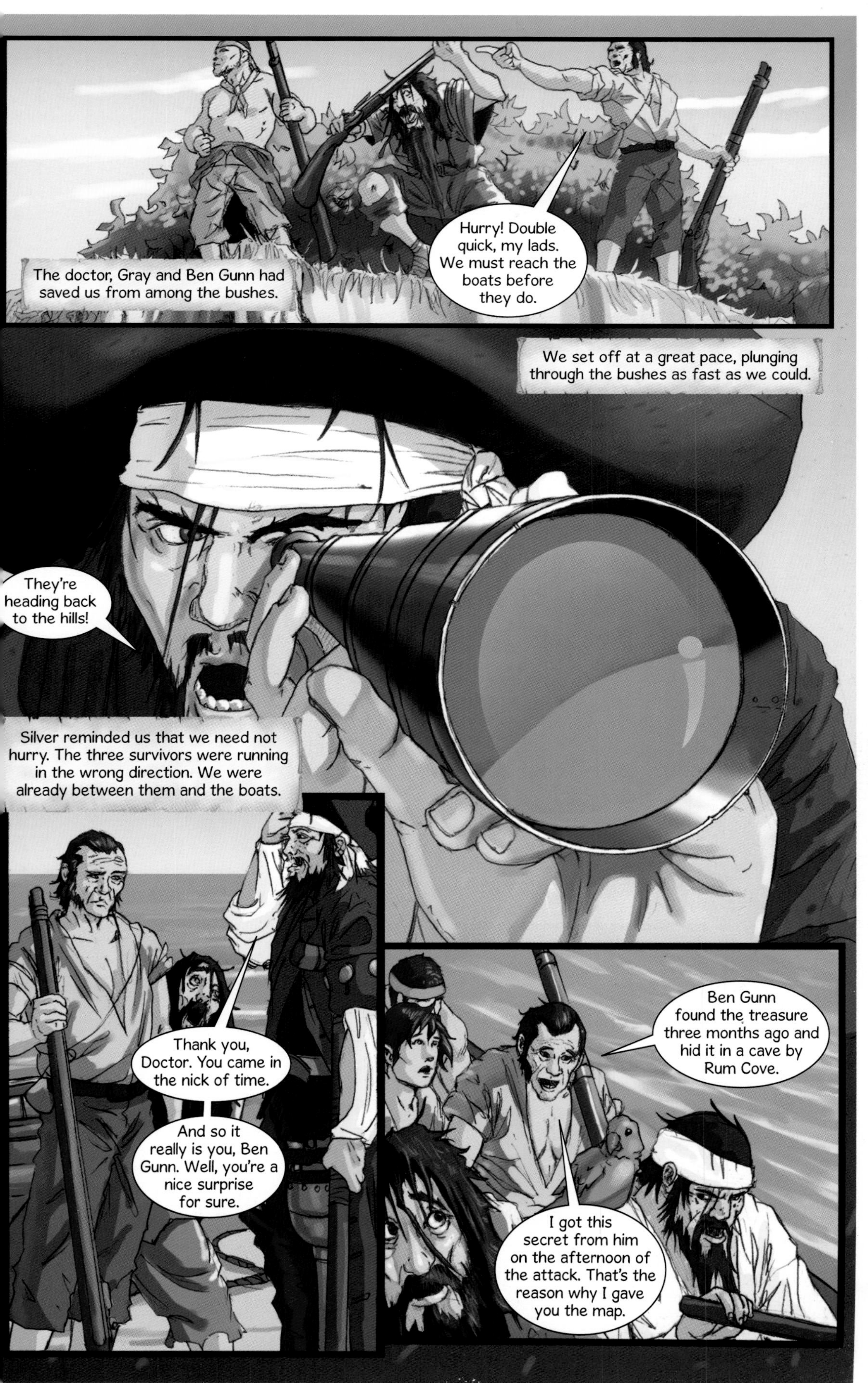

The doctor, Gray and Ben Gunn had saved us from among the bushes.
Hurry! Double quick, my lads. We must reach the boats before they do.
We set off at a great pace, plunging through the bushes as fast as we could.
They're heading back to the hills!
Silver reminded us that we need not hurry. The three survivors were running in the wrong direction. We were already between them and the boats.
Thank you, Doctor. You came in the nick of time.
And so it really is you, Ben Gunn. Well, you're a nice surprise for sure.
Ben Gunn found the treasure three months ago and hid it in a cave by Rum Cove.
I got this secret from him on the afternoon of the attack. That's the reason why I gave you the map.

We made our way back to the cave where Ben Gunn had hidden the treasure.
Welcome back, fellows!
Long John Silver, you're a terrible villain and an imposter. But I've been told not to prosecute you. So, then, I will not.
Thank you, sir.
What brings you here, Silver?
I have come back to do my duty, Captain Smollett.
Ah!
And here was the treasure— heaps of coins, and bars of gold.
Is Mr. Gray coming for dinner?
No. I assigned him guard duty on the *Hispaniola* tonight.

The next day, it was decided that we should leave the three pirates on the island.
None of them will leave this place.
crack
But we'll leave some supplies for them.
For three days, we stowed away the treasure on the ship. We also made sure we took enough water and goat meat for ourselves.
At last, we weighed anchor, leaving the three pirates deserted and pleading with us to save them.
We left a stock of powder and shot, the bulk of the goat meat, a few medicines, some tools, clothing, a spare sail, some rope and, on the insistence of the doctor, some tobacco.
Captain Smollett gave orders to sail for Spanish America.
Good idea. We'll need more hands before we attempt the trip home.

Don't leave us here to die, Silver!
Have mercy on us!
It touched all our hearts to leave them in that state. But we could not risk another revolt.
Fresh flowers for sale!
Fresh fruit!
Around sunset, we reached a most beautiful gulf, and were immediately surrounded by boats full of locals selling fruit and vegetables.
Are you coming ashore, Captain Silver?
I need my rest. Have fun, and bring me back a bottle of wine.
We met an English captain, and went on board his ship.
Jim did make some questionable decisions during our adventure but, at every step, he saved our lives.
What a fantastic tale.
Thanks for your hospitality, Captain Walker.
Day was just breaking when we got back to the *Hispaniola*.
Silver's run away!

Ben Gunn was on deck alone.
I helped him escape only to save your lives. Silver is too dangerous a man to have on board.
But this was not all. Silver had not gone empty-handed.
♪ ♫ Fifteen ♫ men on the dead man's chest...
He had taken one of the sacks of coins, worth perhaps three or four hundred guineas, to help him on his way.
ADMIRAL BENBOW INN
I think we were all pleased to be rid of him so easily.
To cut a long story short, we then got a few hands on board and cruised back home.
We all received a good share of the treasure and used it wisely or foolishly according to our nature.
Mr. Gray not only saved his money but, with his desire to rise, also studied his profession. He is now mate, and part owner, of a fine, fully-equipped ship, besides being married and having children.
Ben Gunn received a thousand pounds, which he lost in three weeks or, to be exact, nineteen days. He was back begging on the twentieth day.

Captain Smollett decided to retire from the sea.
Of Silver, we heard no more.
That formidable seafaring man with one leg has, at last, gone out of my life.
Perhaps he will pay for his misdeeds in the future.
We weren't able to bring all the treasure back, and some of it still lies on the island where Flint buried it. But it can stay there.
Nothing will take me back to that accursed island. The worst dreams I ever have are of the surf booming about its coasts, and I often start upright in bed with the sharp voice of Captain Flint still ringing in my ears...
Pieces of eight! Pieces of eight!

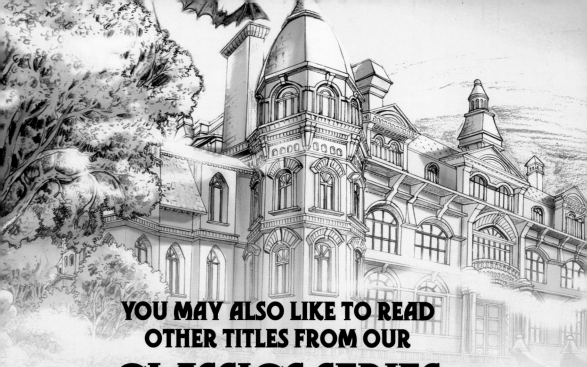

YOU MAY ALSO LIKE TO READ OTHER TITLES FROM OUR CLASSICS SERIES

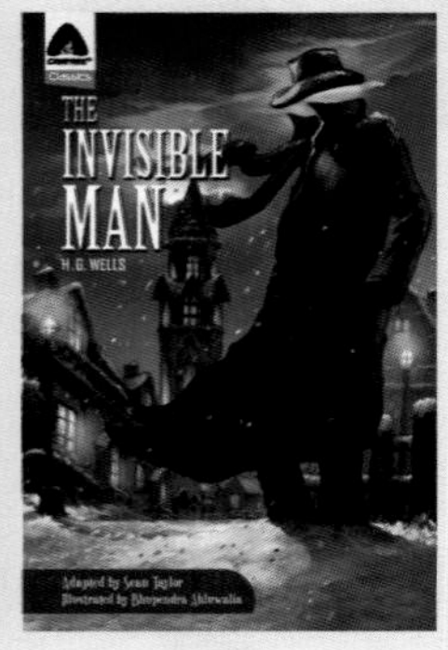

When the residents of Iping first see him, he is wearing an overcoat and goggles, and is covered from head to toe with bandages. They assume he must have been involved in some kind of horrific accident. But as the reality of the situation starts to become clear, only one thing is certain—the stranger is a troubled soul and can only deal with his personal fear by terrorizing the people around him. First published in 1897, *The Invisible Man* is H.G. Wells's warning to the world about the dangers of science without humanity

Without telling his parents, young Robinson sets off on a voyage of discovery. During the years that follow, he learns much, not just about the world, but about himself as well. Following disaster at sea on more than one occasion, Robinson toys with the idea of settling down. However, his adventurous character gets the better of him and he boards ship once again. This time, though, a calamitous shipwreck wipes out the whole of the crew and leaves Crusoe alone on a seemingly deserted island. How is it possible for one man to survive in such a situation? Will he manage to leave or be forced to remain on the island?

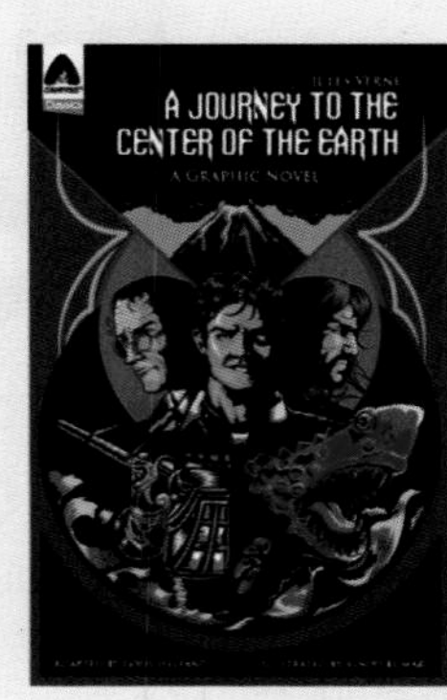

When Sir Charles Baskerville is found dead on the moors, a heart attack seems to be the likely cause. However, a certain Dr. Mortimer thinks there is more to it than that. The unparalleled detective, Sherlock Holmes; his sidekick, Dr. Watson; and an intriguing and mysterious plot make Sir Arthur Conan Doyle's *The Hound of the Baskervilles* a compelling read.

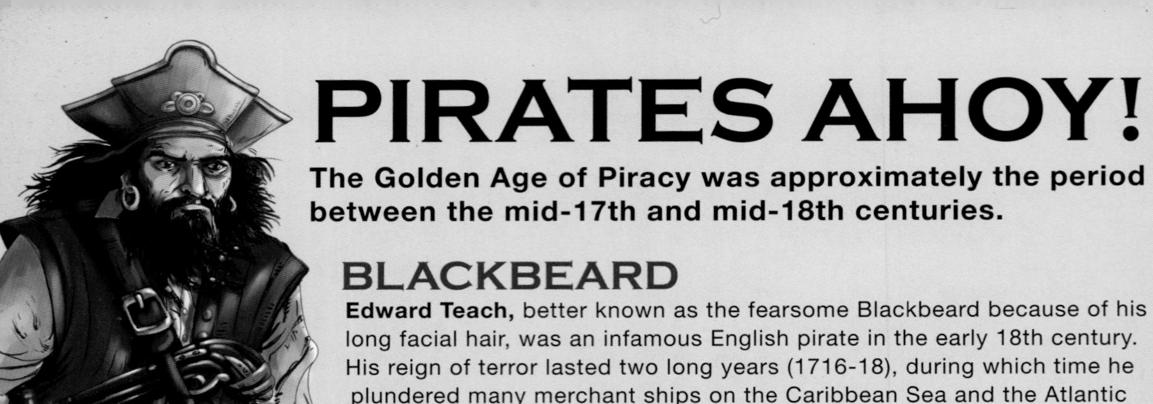

PIRATES AHOY!

The Golden Age of Piracy was approximately the period between the mid-17th and mid-18th centuries.

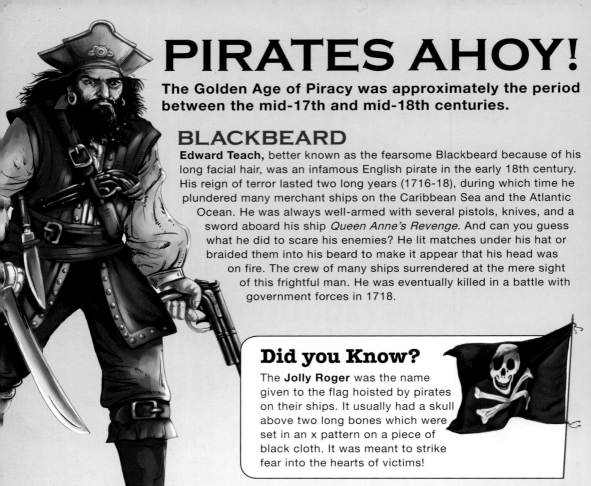

BLACKBEARD

Edward Teach, better known as the fearsome Blackbeard because of his long facial hair, was an infamous English pirate in the early 18th century. His reign of terror lasted two long years (1716-18), during which time he plundered many merchant ships on the Caribbean Sea and the Atlantic Ocean. He was always well-armed with several pistols, knives, and a sword aboard his ship *Queen Anne's Revenge*. And can you guess what he did to scare his enemies? He lit matches under his hat or braided them into his beard to make it appear that his head was on fire. The crew of many ships surrendered at the mere sight of this frightful man. He was eventually killed in a battle with government forces in 1718.

Did you Know?

The **Jolly Roger** was the name given to the flag hoisted by pirates on their ships. It usually had a skull above two long bones which were set in an x pattern on a piece of black cloth. It was meant to strike fear into the hearts of victims!

THE PIRATES' CODE OF CONDUCT

Surprising but true: pirates followed their own set of strict rules. The codes varied from ship to ship, but had a common aim—to keep the crew from doing anything wrong. Some general codes included:

- **All members of the crew would get a fair share of the booty.**
- **A deserter or anyone keeping any secret from the rest would be marooned on an island, or in a small boat, with just some gunpowder, a bottle of water, and a gun with one bullet.**
- **A lazy man, or one who failed to keep his weapons clean, would lose his share of the booty.**
- **Every member would get a share of any captured drink and fresh food.**
- **Gambling was forbidden.**
- **Every member was compensated for the loss of a leg or hand in battle.**

CAPTAIN KIDD

A British pirate, **William Kidd,** became known as one of the most infamous outlaws of all time. He plundered ships along the coast of North America, the Caribbean and the Indian Ocean in the 17th century, and accumulated a great deal of wealth. It is believed that **Captain Kidd** buried treasure from the plundered ship, *Quedagh Merchant,* on Gardiner's Island in the U.S.A., before he was executed in 1701. Though some of it was found, legend has it that a large quantity still remains undiscovered. Over the years, many people have searched for it in vain. Treasure hunters have even gone down to the depths of the ocean in the hope of discovering the notorious pirate's great treasure.

PIRATE SHIPS

Contrary to popular depictions, pirates generally used small and speedy ships rather than huge galleons. Two of the most popular ships in the Golden Age of Piracy were sloops and schooners:

Did you Know?

Pirates often fell sick because of the lack of good food. Scurvy, a disease caused by the lack of vitamin C, was a common ailment. Pirates knew they had it when their teeth started falling out and their skin began to go pale!

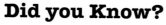

SLOOPS

Light and maneuverable, **sloops** had shallow draughts which helped them sail into shallow waters to escape from, or chase, other ships. They could sail quickly, even without any wind, and with just a few pairs of oars. They were relatively small and usually contained up to 75 men and 14 guns.

SCHOONERS

Fast-moving ships, **schooners** had narrow hulls that allowed them to navigate easily over shoals and shallow waters. They had the capacity to take a full load and the 75-man crew inland, to hide in caves or to divide the pirates' spoils. Captain Smollett's ship, *Hispaniola,* is a schooner.

Other Titles by

ROBERT LOUIS STEVENSON

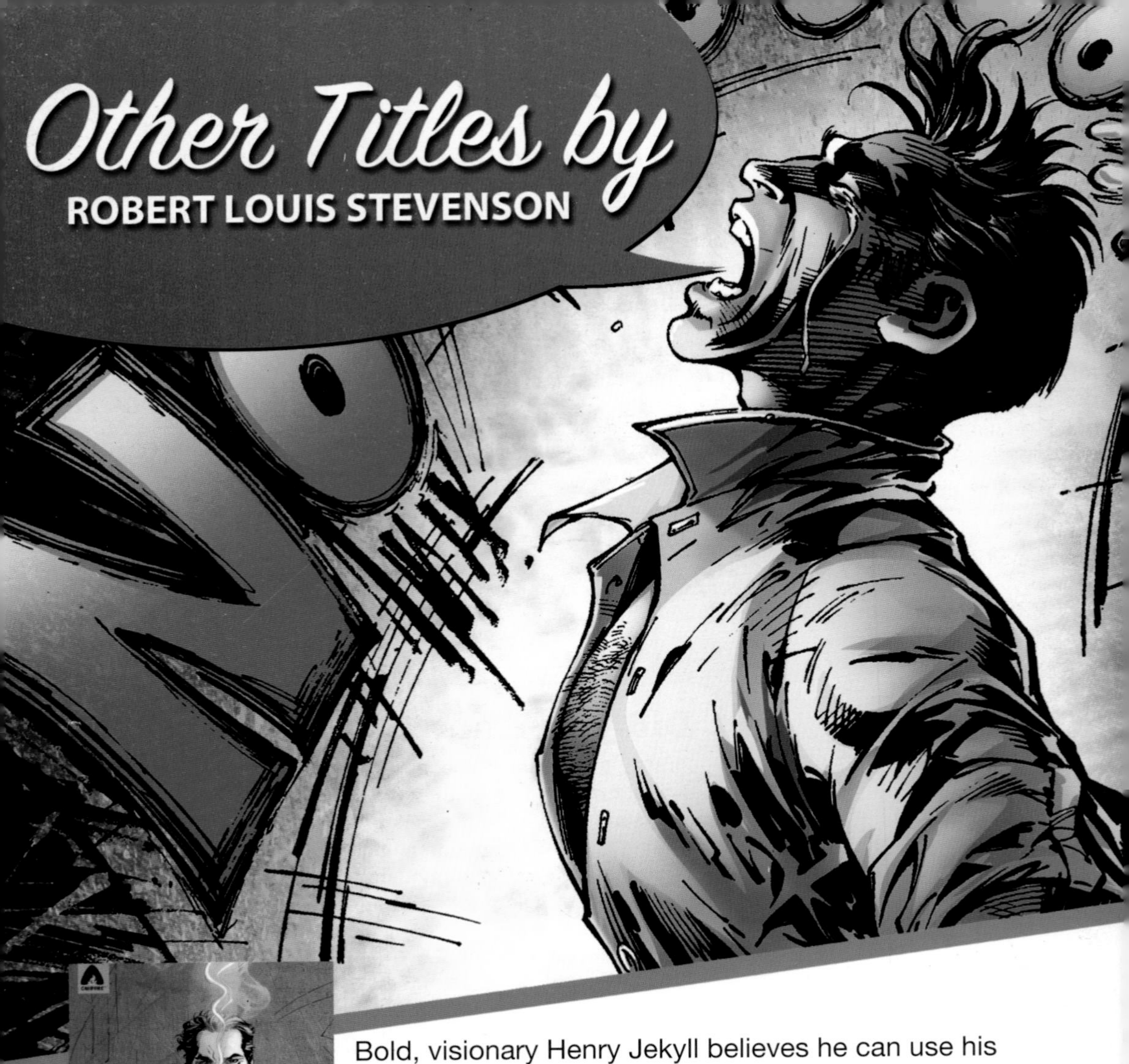

Bold, visionary Henry Jekyll believes he can use his scientific knowledge to divide a person into two beings—one of pure good and one of pure evil. Working tirelessly in his secret laboratory he eventually succeeds—but only halfway. Instead of separating the good and evil halves, Jekyll manages to isolate only the latter. His friends think Jekyll will waste away and fear the worst. Can Jekyll undo what he has done? Or will it change things forever?

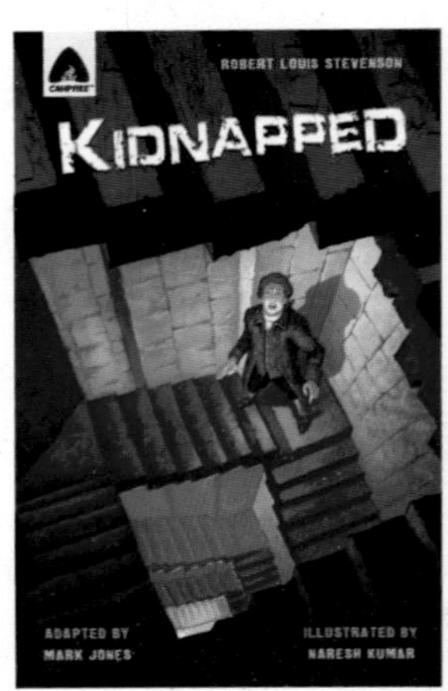

When David Balfour approaches his uncle Ebenezer to claim his inheritance, little is he aware of his uncle's plans for his future. Bound, gagged and left on a ship, David Balfour finds out that he is to be sold at the American Colonies. Accused of a murder he didn't commit, David finds himself travelling the wild highlands with an unlikely companion, the revolutionary Jacobite Alan Breck. From artfully dodging Redcoats to playing the bagpipes, the duo will do anything to survive! But will they? Find out!